Disney
Fairies

Rani
in the
Mermaid
Lagoon

Rani
in the
Mermaid
Lagoon

WRITTEN BY
LISA PAPADEMETRIOU

ILLUSTRATED BY
THE DISNEY STORYBOOK ARTISTS

HarperCollins *Children's Books*

First published in the USA by Disney Press,
114 Fifth Avenue, New York, New York, 10011-5690.

First published in Great Britain in 2006
by HarperCollins Children's Books.
HarperCollins Children's Books is a division of
HarperCollins Publishers,
77 - 85 Fulham Palace Road, Hammersmith, London, W6 8JB.

The HarperCollins Children's Books website is
www.harpercollinschildrensbooks.co.uk

978-0-00-720934-7

0-00-720934-7

1 2 3 4 5 6 7 8 9 10

Printed and bound in Great Britain by Clays Ltd,
St Ives plc.

Visit disneyfairies.com

All About Fairies

IF YOU HEAD toward the second star on your right and fly straight on till morning, you'll come to Never Land, a magical island where mermaids play and children never grow up.

When you arrive, you might hear something like the tinkling of little bells. Follow that sound and you'll find Pixie Hollow, the secret heart of Never Land.

A great old maple tree grows in Pixie Hollow, and in it live hundreds of fairies and sparrow men. Some of them can do water magic, others can fly like the wind, and still others can speak to animals. You see, Pixie Hollow is the Never fairies' kingdom, and each fairy who lives there has a special, extraordinary talent.

Not far from the Home Tree, nestled in the branches of a hawthorn, is Mother Dove, the most magical creature of all. She sits on her egg, watching over the fairies, who in turn watch over her. For as long as Mother Dove's egg stays well and whole, no one in Never Land will ever grow old.

Once, Mother Dove's egg *was* broken. But we are not telling the story of the egg here. Now it is time for Rani's tale...

Rani
in the
Mermaid
Lagoon

1

Rani paused at the gleaming metal door to Tinker Bell's workshop. She bit her lip. *I'm not going to cry*, she told herself. *This time, I'm not.* Rani could hear her friend hammering away inside the teapot. Tink was busy, as usual.

Tink was a pots-and-pans-talent fairy, and the best fixer in Pixie Hollow. She could fix almost anything – a ladle that leaked, a stubborn pot that never boiled, a colander that refused to let water run through its holes. Rani was hoping that Tink could fix her problem.

Rani took a deep breath and walked into her friend's workshop. "Hi, Tink," she said.

With an impatient frown, Tinker Bell looked up from the copper pot she had been hammering. But when she saw Rani, she smiled, showing her dimples. "Rani!" she said. She put down her hammer. "What are you doing here? Why aren't you – "

" – making the fountain?" Rani finished. She did that sometimes – got excited and finished other fairies' sentences for them. "It's because – " Rani stopped. "Because – " She tried again, but she didn't get any further before she burst into tears.

"Rani, what's wrong?" Tink flew over to her friend and patted her gently on the back. Her fingers avoided the place where Rani's wings used to be. Rani was a wingless fairy – the only one in Pixie Hollow. She had cut off her wings to save Never Land. That made her a hero. It also made her the only fairy who couldn't fly on her own. A bird named Brother Dove helped her when she needed him.

On the other hand, Rani was the only fairy in Pixie Hollow who could swim. Fairy wings become very, very heavy when they are wet. That's why fairies never swim – they'd get dragged under the water. And as a water-talent fairy, Rani *adored* water.

Rani pulled out a damp leafkerchief and blew her nose. Another crystal tear trickled down her face. "Tonight is the Fairy Dance," she began.

Tink grabbed a handful of fresh leaf-kerchiefs. She always kept some handy in case water-talent fairies came to visit. "I can't wait," she said.

The Fairy Dance was the reason she had been working so hard to fix the copper pot. The cooking-talent fairies needed it right away. The pot had recently decided it was a skillet, and served up stack after stack of pancakes, no matter what the cook was trying to make. But the cooking-talent fairies couldn't serve pancakes at the most important party of the month! Frowning, Tink tapped the pot with her tinker's hammer, but the dent in its side stubbornly refused to budge.

The Fairy Dance was held once every full moon. That was when the moon was at its fattest, brightest, and merriest. All the talents worked together to make the party the best it could be. The light-talent fairies hung glowworms from the branches of the Home Tree. They also set fireflies loose over the clearing where the dance was held. The baking-talent fairies made stacks of sweet, crisp butter cookies. The cooking-talent fairies made crustless mushroom sandwiches as light as a feather, and acorn caps full of pumpkin soup. The decoration-talent fairies made sure the leaves of the maple trees in Pixie Hollow sparkled. And the water-talent fairies made a fountain at the center of the clearing. The fountain was important because all the fairies danced around it.

Just thinking about the fountain made Rani burst into tears again. She wiped them away impatiently and took a deep breath. "You know I always make the large water jet that goes at the very top of the Fairy Dance fountain," she started to explain.

"Of course you do," Tink said. "You make the prettiest jet in all of Pixie Hollow."

"Well, the other water-talent fairies think Humidia should do it." Tears filled Rani's eyes once more. Her nose began to run. "Because I can't fly. They said Brother Dove's flapping wings would mess up the shape of the jet when I placed it at the top of the fountain.

They said his wings would probably destroy the whole fountain if we went too close!"

Tink tugged on her fringe. She knew how it felt to think you might be losing your talent. It felt *awful*. "The fountain won't be the same without your talent. That's – "

" – terrible," Rani finished, shaking her head. "I'm a water-talent fairy, and I can't even help with the water fountain!"

Rani squeezed her leafkerchief, dripping water onto the floor. She dabbed at her overflowing eyes again. Water-talent fairies are as full of liquid as a ripe, juicy berry. They perspire, cry, and sniffle more than other fairies. They just can't help it.

"Well," Tink said, "whether or not you work on the fountain, it's still a party. And you *love* parties. I'll save you a spot in the Fairy Dance. Until then, maybe you can use your talent to help another talent."

"Another talent?" Rani repeated. She pressed her lips together, thinking hard. "I can help the cooking-talent fairies boil the water," she said. She had done that once or twice before. It wasn't as much fun as working on the fountain, but it was better than nothing. In fact, maybe she could help the cooking-talent fairies make something delicious to eat. That would be fun, Rani realised. "Thanks, Tink. I'll go ask right now," she said as she hurried out the door.

"Don't mention it!" Tink called.

But Rani didn't hear her. She was on her way to the kitchen.

Rani stood at the edge of the fairy circle and sighed. She had already been to the huge kitchen in the Home Tree. She had asked if she could help the cooking-talent fairies boil water. But they had told Rani that the food was already prepared. Then Rani had come to the clearing to see if she could help another talent. But everything was already done. There was nothing left for her to do.

A long table was heaped with all sorts of treats the cooking- and baking-talent fairies had whipped up. There were cream tarts, sticky muffins, and platters of mushroom sandwiches. The polishing-talent fairies had shined the forks, spoons, and knives until they gleamed. The table-setting-talent fairies were putting them out. The gardening-talent fairies had cleared the grounds and planted bright blue pansies around the edges. The light-talent fairies had already placed the glowworms. The fireflies were gathering nearby.

"Moon and stars! The fountain looks

beautiful, Rani," said a voice.

Rani turned and saw Fira smiling at her. Her eyes were twinkling. Fira, also known as Moth, was a light-talent fairy. She glowed more brightly than a normal Never fairy. Even the tips of her long, dark hair sparkled.

Fira looked back at the fountain. She paused thoughtfully. Fira often considered her words carefully before she spoke. "I just wish I could find a way to light it up," she said finally. "But whenever I try to get a flame near the water, it – "

" – goes out, I know," Rani agreed.

"Still, it looks very good," Fira said.

Rani sighed. "Thanks, but I didn't have anything to do with it. I can't fly, so Humidia took my job."

"Oh, Rani," Fira said.

Rani turned away. Tears prickled in her

eyes... again.

"Try not to worry," Fira said. "You'll go to the dance tonight and have a wonderful time." She snapped, and a spark flew from her fingers. It swirled above their heads for a moment, then blinked out. "Dancing will help you forget all about the fountain."

Rani looked into Fira's smiling dark eyes, which shone with happy pinpoints of light. She knew Fira was trying to help. Rani gave her a watery smile.

Fira could see that her friend was still feeling sad. "Don't forget that you saved Mother Dove's egg," Fira pointed out. "You have more than one talent, Rani."

But there's only one talent I want, Rani thought. Still, she knew there was no point in arguing. Humidia had made the fountain's jet. That was all there was to it. Now Rani had to try to enjoy the Fairy Dance as well as she could.

"Thanks, Fira," Rani said after a moment. "I'll see you tonight at the dance."

2

"DOWN THERE, BROTHER Dove!" Rani said excitedly. She leaned forward to peer over Brother Dove's neck as he swooped toward the fairy circle.

The fireflies winked. They – along with the glowworms – sent a soft light through the clearing. The fairy fountain sparkled at the center. It was tall, rising almost as high as the trunk of the sycamore that stood nearby. The music-talent fairies were already tuning their grass-reed instruments. Rani bit her lip. She was a little late.

Brother Dove started toward a spot just under the trees where several branches met. Stars twinkled in the gaps between the leaves. Fairies flitted about, forming three circles and practicing their cartwheels for the dance. Even nasty Vidia smiled as she watched from a short distance away.

"There she is!" Rani cried. She had spotted Tink hovering between Beck, an animal-talent fairy, and Terence, a dust-talent sparrow man.

Just then, the music-talent fairies struck up the first notes of the Fairy Dance melody.

"Hurry!" Rani cried. "The dance is starting!" She wanted to take her usual place near Tink in the outer circle.

There were three circles in the Fairy Dance. All three circled in midair around the fairy fountain. The inner circle was the smallest and the easiest to dance in. The youngest fairies danced in this circle until they learned the dance. Then there was a middle circle. That was for fairies who knew the dance but weren't experts. The outer circle was the largest. It was also the hardest to dance in. There was a lot of twirling, flipping, and cartwheeling.

Sometimes, the outer-circle dancers changed direction and danced in the opposite way from the fairies in the middle circle. It was like what Clumsies called a square dance, only it was round. It was also much more difficult. All three circles were in constant motion, moving one way and then another and switching dancers.

Rani loved dancing in the outer circle. A fairy had to dance very quickly to keep up with the music. If she didn't keep up, she lost her place in the circle. Then she had to wait until the next song to dance again. This time, however, it would be different for Rani – she'd be on Brother Dove's back.

Brother Dove flew toward the outer circle

of fairies. Luckily, there was no breeze that night. A gust of wind could make the dancers bump into each other.

"Rani! Over here!" Tink called. She and Beck flipped from the outer circle to the center circle, then out again. Terence was right beside Tink. *He's going to crash into someone if he isn't careful,* Rani thought. *He's paying more attention to Tink than to the other dancers around him!*

With two quick flaps of his wings, Brother Dove shot toward where Tink was doing a midair flip. But the musicians had reached the fastest part of the song. The fairies' wings were moving so fast they were humming.

"Fly me here!" the fairies sang as everyone turned a cartwheel to the left. *Clap-clap-clap!* "Fly me there!" Cartwheel to the right, and *clap-clap-clap!*

Rani knew she should be grateful to Brother Dove even to be a part of the Fairy Dance. But she couldn't help feeling left out as the other fairies flipped and zipped from one circle to the next. Since Brother Dove was so much bigger than the fairies, he kept to the outer circle. Still, it was nice to join in the dance...

"Whoa!" Rani cried. She stopped clapping to hold tightly to the soft, downy feathers at Brother Dove's neck as he did a little flip of his own. "Over there!" Rani pointed to the far side of the outer circle. Tink had flipped out of the inner circle and was now on the other side.

Rani stood up as Brother Dove flapped toward Tink. This was her favourite part of the dance. Kick and kick, then jump, jump, jump!

A light little leap, then twirl to your right...

My *feet haven't forgotten*, Rani thought. She started to move in time to the music. *I may not have wings, but I can still dance!* Rani grinned and twirled to her right –

Oh, no!

With a cry, Rani felt her foot slip from Brother Dove's back. She flailed her arms. A moment later, she plunged into empty space.

"Rani!" Tinker Bell shouted. She dove after her friend.

"Tink!" Terence cried. Around him, the dance turned into a jumble. Fairies crashed into each other.

The green grass of the clearing rushed up to meet Rani as she fell toward the ground. She didn't even have time to scream before she felt a yank on her arm. Her fall slowed slightly.

"Thanks, Tink!" Rani said with a gasp. But Tink wasn't strong enough to stop her. Now they were both falling.

There was another dreadful yank as Terence caught Tink under the arms and struggled to hold her up.

Screams and gasps came from the fairies. Terence, Tink, and Rani crashed through the fountain, shattering it. Water showered everywhere. But they were moving more slowly now. Seconds later, Fira caught Rani's other arm. The strength of all three fairies was enough. They set Rani down gently on the soft green grass.

For a moment, everything was silent. Rani looked around at the wreck she had caused. There was a floating knot of fairies whose wings had gotten tangled up. A sparrow man had plunged facefirst into a pot of pumpkin soup. One of Terence's wings was bent, and half of Tink's hair had come loose from her ponytail. All that was left of the fountain was a damp puddle on the grass. Rani's brand-new violet-petal dress was torn.

The musicians were quiet. The only sound Rani could hear was the beat of Brother Dove's wings as he landed beside her.

Tink's large blue eyes looked worried. "Rani, are you okay?"

Rani felt the hot tears begin to flow down her face. She whispered, "I didn't mean to - "

"Didn't mean to?" a voice interrupted. Cruel Vidia - the fastest of the fast-flying-talent fairies - flew down to land beside Rani. Tinker Bell folded her arms across her chest and glared at Vidia.

"Darling, you must understand that we're all simply *worried* about you," Vidia went on with a touch too much sugar in her voice. Her red lips curled into a smile. "Why, a fairy with no wings couldn't *hope* to be a part of the Fairy Dance," Vidia said. "I'm surprised you even tried."

"Be quiet, Vidia," Fira snapped. "She was doing fine until – "

"Until she ruined the entire thing, including her own talent's fountain?" Vidia finished. "Sweetie, it isn't your fault that you wrecked the dance," she said to Rani. "We all understand that you were only   trying to belong. But you have to accept the fact that without your wings, you're useless."

"Vidia – " Tink growled. She balled her tiny fists in rage.

But Rani didn't hear the end of Tink's sentence. She had already started running. She didn't stop even when she heard Tinker Bell calling her name.

3

RANI SAT BENEATH a tall willow tree, weeping. She cried until there was a puddle all around her. She cried until she had no more tears left. This had never happened to Rani before. She'd always been full of water.

When her sobs ended, the dark woods were silent. Rani was in a part of the forest she didn't know. "I should go back to the Home Tree," she said aloud. Her voice skipped between the trees and disappeared into the blackness of the night. Rani took a step toward the Home Tree. She could picture its comforting branches, the brightly lit rooms full of fairies.

Rani sighed. "They don't want me," she said, feeling sorry for herself. But where else could she go? "Well," she reasoned, "I can't go back. So I might as well go forward." And with that, she turned and walked farther into the woods.

Past the tall, dark trees and beyond a moonlit clearing, Rani came to a little trickling branch of Havendish Stream. She picked up a small pebble and dropped it into the water. Then she walked to the edge of the stream and stepped in up to her ankles.

The cool, clear water ran over her tired feet. She felt her mood lift. With a kick, Rani splashed a frog that was sitting by the side of the stream. She laughed as he croaked and flopped into the water.

Rani splashed around a little longer, then made her way back to shore. She was just about to step out of the stream when she saw it – a pretty little birch-bark canoe. Water-talent fairies sometimes used them to go exploring. This one looked as if it had been swept downstream when a careless fairy didn't tie it up properly.

"It's almost as though someone left it here for me," Rani said to herself.

A paddle lay in a puddle of water in the bottom of the canoe. Rani moved her hand over the puddle. In a moment, the water formed a ball. Rani picked it up and tossed it into the river, where it dissolved into the rest of the water. She ran her hands over the whole boat, making sure it was watertight. Then she stepped into the canoe.

Moonlight sparkled on the water as Rani paddled downstream. A small waterfall whispered gently. Rani didn't know where she was going. As long as it was away from the other fairies, it was fine with her.

Peeking over the edge of the canoe, Rani

looked down at her small, heart-shaped face reflected in the water. *From the front, I still look like a normal fairy,* she thought. She reached out and touched the water. Her face dissolved into ripples.

Rani cupped water in her hand and brought it to her lips. "Good-bye, Tinker Bell," she whispered into the water. "I'll miss you. You are my forever friend, but I can't stay with the fairies anymore."

She blew on the water, and it grew and stretched until it was a large bubble. Rani lifted her hand into the air. The bubble shimmered in front of her for a moment before it floated away. A breeze pushed it toward the Home Tree, where it would find Tink. Rani had sent many of these bubble messages before. They never failed.

With a sigh, Rani leaned back. She

watched the stars overhead as the canoe carried her downstream. She saw a long, moss-covered log lying across the stream, like a bridge. Just as Rani's canoe passed under the log, she heard a soft splash.

What was that? Rani wondered. She sat up in the canoe. Looking over the side, she saw a whiplike motion in the dark water behind her. It was a water snake!

Rani's heart fluttered in her chest. Snakes were almost as dangerous to fairies as hawks were. She dipped her paddle in the water, straining with all her might. The canoe started to pull away. A glance backward told her that the snake was moving quickly.

"Hurry, hurry!" Rani urged herself. The canoe sped forward. Suddenly, Rani heard a soft hissing sound.

She turned, expecting the snake to be

right on top of her. But he was still several canoe lengths away.

Startled, Rani faced forward. The hissing she heard wasn't the snake. It was the hiss water makes as it races over rocks. "Oh, no!" Rani cried. She dug her paddle into the water, trying to slow the canoe.

Hiss!

Behind her, the water snake drew level with the canoe. He was going to strike! "Get back!" Rani shouted. She stood and raised her paddle.

In a flash, the snake lunged forward. Rani brought her paddle down on his head. The snake bent under the force of the blow, then pulled back. His forked tongue flickered in and out. His black eyes narrowed in fury.

Rani thought fast. When the snake struck, she held back for an extra moment.

Just as the snake's fangs were about to close over her, she shoved her paddle between his jaws.

The snake thrashed from side to side. Water splashed wildly, but the paddle didn't budge. He couldn't close his mouth!

Rani started to relax. But then she remembered that she had another problem. The hiss had become a roar.

Turning toward the front of the canoe, Rani saw the white water just ahead. She grabbed the side of the boat. It swayed and rocked. Rani let out a scream. Her ears were filled with the noise of the rapids. Her stomach felt sick from the motion.

I can't hang on! Rani thought. Her hand slipped from the side of the canoe.

The canoe hit the largest rock in the rapids. The boat ripped apart with the force of the blow. Rani was tossed into the water.

She struggled against the current, but it was too strong. Finally, she gave up and let the water swallow her.

4

"I KNOW WHAT this is... I've seen one before. It's a fairy."

"It can't be a fairy. It doesn't have a wand. Or wings."

"Not all fairies have wands, you know."

"Yes, they do."

"Shhh! It's moving."

Rani coughed. Her eyes fluttered open. At first, all she could see was a bright light and a shadow. Finally, the world came into focus. Someone was looking down at her curiously. She had beautiful green eyes, a delicate nose, yellow-green hair – and skin made of tiny scales.

A *mermaid!* Rani thought. A second mermaid with blue eyes and blue-green hair was beside the first one.

Rani sat up, then wished she hadn't moved so quickly. Her whole body was sore. As she looked around, she saw that she was lying on the shore. The mermaids leaned over her with their tails still in the water.

"Where am I?" Rani asked.

"She wants to know where she is," the blue-eyed mermaid said.

"I heard her," the green-eyed one snapped. She looked down at Rani. "You're where Havendish Stream meets the Mermaid Lagoon," she told Rani.

"Are you a fairy?" the other one asked.

Rani coughed again. "Yes."

"There," the green-eyed mermaid said in a haughty way. "Didn't I tell you? They don't *all* have wands."

Rani looked at the green-eyed mermaid carefully. "I think I know you," she said.

"Aren't you... Soop?"

The mermaid smiled. Soop's name wasn't really Soop, but only other mermaids could pronounce her real name. "I'm not Soop," she said. "Though creatures who don't know better think we look alike. I'm Oola. And who are you?"

"I'm Rani."

"If you're a fairy," the other mermaid said, "where are your wings?"

"Oh, be quiet, Mara," Oola grumbled. (Mara wasn't the other mermaid's name either, but it was the only part Rani could catch.) "Isn't it obvious? She cut them off so that she could swim with mermaids."

Mara's eyes widened. "You did?"

"Well... " Rani had cut off her wings because she'd needed to ask the mermaids for one of their beautiful combs to save Mother

Dove's egg. So in a way, she *had* cut off her wings to swim with mermaids. "... yes. I guess so."

Mara gasped in admiration. She looked Rani over from head to toe. Rani blushed again. She knew she was a mess. Her blonde hair was tangled, and her violet dress – already torn from her fall at the Fairy Dance – was now practically in rags. "So," Mara said, "what are you doing – "

" – here?" Rani shook her head. "I'm running away."

The mermaids gasped. "Running away!" Oola repeated.

"I would never leave the Mermaid Lagoon," Mara said.

"Mara!" Oola snapped. "Don't insult the fairy. Not everyone lives in a place as nice as the Mermaid Lagoon."

"Oh, Pixie Hollow is beautiful," Rani put in quickly.

Oola smiled. But she didn't look as though she believed Rani. "Of course it is."

Rani couldn't think of anything to say after that.

Oola flicked her yellow-green tail thoughtfully as Rani toyed with a handful of water. Cupping it in her palms, Rani turned the drop into a ball, then stretched it so that it had a forked tongue and a long tail. She breathed on it, and the water snake's tail flickered.

"How did you do that?" Oola asked.

Rani shrugged. "I'm a water-talent fairy," she explained. "Water is my joy."

Reaching out a finger, Oola touched the water snake. It melted right away, falling back into the stream with a tiny splash. Oola laughed. "I guess I don't have any water talent," she said.

"Mermaids have different talents," Rani said, thinking about how graceful and lovely Oola and Mara were.

"Where will you go now?" Mara asked.

Rani sighed. "I don't know," she admitted.

Leaning over, Oola whispered something in Mara's ear. Mara's blue eyes widened, and she whispered something back to Oola. Oola nodded.

"We think you should come and live with us," Oola told Rani.

"You'd like it," Mara agreed.

"Me?" Rani flushed with pride. These beautiful mermaids wanted her to live with them? Underwater? The fairy's heart fluttered with excitement.

"You seem very happy in water," Oola pointed out.

Rani's smile faded. "But I can't breathe underwater," she said. To *live* underwater she would need a lot of air. Then Rani remembered the bubble message she had made for Tink. Couldn't she make a few bubbles like that and wear them as a necklace? Anytime she wanted to breathe, she could just pop one in her mouth –

"And take a breath!" Rani said aloud. She was so excited that she stood straight up.

Oola held out her hand, and Rani stepped onto it. "You'll be like a tiny mermaid," Oola said. She kindly ignored the fact that Rani didn't have scales... or a tail.

Rani smiled. She was off on an underwater adventure!

5

RANI LOOKED AROUND in amazement as they made their way through the mermaid lagoon.

A cloud of brilliant silver-blue fish darted past, and Rani saw three mermaids sitting on a rock. A merman inspected a field of bright green seaweed – he was the palace chef and was gathering salad greens. Two small merboys chased each other through a patch of coral.

"How much farther to the castle?" Rani asked Oola. They had already been swimming for quite a while. Rani was thankful that she had thought of the bubble necklace. It was easy to breathe that way. Every time she put a bubble in her mouth, it was like taking a gulp of air. And if all else failed, she could always use the wind room.

The wind room was a room full of air

that the mermaids used when their gills got tired. Unfortunately, the room reeked of fish. And Rani couldn't take the room with her if she wanted to leave the mermaid palace. All in all, the bubble necklace made it much easier to stay underwater. "It isn't far," Oola replied. "You'll be able to see it once we swim over this hill."

Rani gasped when she caught sight of the castle. The mermaids' palace was made of mother-of-pearl. It gleamed in the sparkling underwater light. To Rani, it seemed huge. It reached from the floor of the lagoon halfway to the surface.

Rani had always thought that the Home Tree was the most beautiful place on earth, but now she wasn't so sure.

"And you all live there?" Rani asked.

"Every mermaid and merman has a room

in the palace," Oola told her.

Now, you might be wondering how it was that Rani and Oola were talking underwater. It was really quite easy if you had a mermaid to show you how to do it. The trick wasn't in the talking... it was in the *listening*. Rani had to listen very carefully to each bubble that came out of Oola's mouth. It took a bit of practice, but once Rani knew how, it was as simple as talking with the fairies in Pixie Hollow.

Oola and Mara swam through the castle. From her seat in Oola's hand, Rani admired everything. In every room, there were bunches of flowering seaweed arranged in tall pink spiral shells. In one room, two large hermit crabs chased each other playfully around a bed made from a giant clamshell.

Throughout the castle, conch shells hid lights that gave off a golden glow. Rani wondered what the lights were made of. They were very pretty.

"Let's go to the dressing room," Mara suggested. "The others will probably be there."

"Oh, let's not," Oola snapped. She was beginning to think of Rani as *her* fairy, and she didn't want to share her with the others. But Voona – a mermaid with a wild mane of yellow-orange hair – caught sight of them.

"Oooh, what do you have there?" Voona asked. She swam right up to Oola and stared at Rani. Her golden eyes widened. "Oh, my goodness – wherever did you get it? It's so strange!"

"I'm Rani," said Rani.

Voona shrieked. "It talks!"

"She's a fairy," Oola explained.

"She is? Where is her wand?" Voona demanded. "Oh, my goodness, we have to show the others right away!" She half pulled, half shoved Oola through a nearby door. "Girls! Girls! Look what we found!"

Soon, a cluster of chattering mermaids surrounded Rani.

"Oh, my gosh! What *is* it?"

"Is it *alive?*"

"How peculiar!"

"It's a fairy," Mara said proudly.

"It *is?*" The mermaids gaped at Rani, who blushed.

"Oh, look – it's turning red," Voona said.

Rani wished the mermaids wouldn't talk about her as though she weren't there. *But how do I ask them to stop without being rude?* she wondered.

Finally, Oola stepped in. "She's a fairy, and she's come to live with us... me. See? She cut off her wings to swim with the mermaids."

Oola pointed to the place where Rani's wings used to be.

The mermaids gasped.

"And," Mara added, "she's had an adventure!"

"No wonder she looks such a mess," Voona said.

Rani blushed even harder, remembering her torn dress. She knew she wasn't looking her best.

"We can dress her up!" one of the mermaids cried.

"Oh, yes! Oh, yes!" the other mermaids agreed. There was a general bustle as they swam to different corners of the room. Each one collected something to help.

Rani sat at the center of a tall table. Mara began to brush her hair. Meanwhile, Oola pulled out a turquoise sea-silk handkerchief and started to make a new dress for Rani. A mermaid with violet hair painted Rani's lips with coral lip gloss.

Another mermaid found a tiny bone pin with a sparkly red jewel at the top. The mermaid took a pin that was similar – only much, much larger – and tied up her own hair with it. Then she told Rani to do the same. Rani did the best she could, but she was sure her hair didn't look as pretty as the mermaid's.

"Oh, much better!" Voona clapped her hands. "This fairy is absolutely adorable – I have to get one!"

Rani smiled as she looked down at the sea-silk dress. It was the most beautiful thing she had ever worn. "Thank you," she said to her new friends.

"That was fun," Oola said.

Rani touched the red jewel in her hair.

She had never had anything so fancy before. "Is there going to be a party?" she asked.

The mermaids stared at her.

"A par-tee?" Voona repeated.

"What's that?" Oola asked.

"A party," Rani said. "You know, where you and your friends dance and play music and eat and have a good time?"

"Sounds like fun!" Mara chirped.

"Oh, it is fun!" Rani said eagerly. "It's very fun!"

"I could wear my new shell necklace!" Mara cried.

"And I could wear my pearl comb," said another mermaid. Immediately, all the mermaids began to plan what to wear.

"Oh!" Oola suddenly wailed. "Oh – it's too terrible!"

"What is it, Oola?" Mara asked. The

other mermaids fell quiet.

"I couldn't possibly think of going to a par-tee without my golden ring!" Oola wailed.

The mermaids were silent.

"Where is it?" Rani asked.

"I dropped it," Oola said, "down Starfish Gap."

The other mermaids murmured and shook their heads.

"It's a very deep, narrow gap," Oola explained. "I'll never get it back." She sighed loudly. She looked at Rani. Then she sighed again.

Rani looked around at the roomful of sad mermaids. It seemed as if the party would never happen now. "Well... ," she said slowly, "... maybe I could go get it."

"Yes!" Mara cried. "Yes, Rani is small enough to fit in the gap!"

"Oh, would you?" Oola exclaimed. "That would be wonderful!"

The mermaids need me, Rani thought with a smile. *They need my help to get the ring. They don't even know how to have a party. I'll have to show them what to do!* "And then we can have our party?" she asked.

"Yes, of course!" Oola promised.

"Well, then," Rani said bravely, "just show me where it is."

6

"ARE YOU SURE it's in there?" Rani asked. She studied the deep, narrow crack in the ocean floor. It was so dark, she couldn't see more than two feet down.

"Oh, yes," Oola assured her. "I dropped it here last week."

"I saw it fall in," Mara added. "It was right by this yellow rock."

Rani hesitated. "It's very dark down there."

"Oh, don't worry about that," Voona said. "We'll hold up this light for you." She held out a conch shell filled with glowing pink seaweed.

Rani stepped forward uncertainly. The light did help, at least a little. She could see that Starfish Gap was lined with plants and corals. It didn't look as though there was anything dangerous down there. Still, it was a strange place, and Rani couldn't see all the way to the bottom. "Are you sure you need this ring?" she asked.

"I couldn't think of going to a par-tee without it," Oola said.

Rani sighed. It was clear she was going to have to get the ring. She plucked a particularly large bubble from her necklace and popped it into her mouth, taking a deep breath. Then she dove over the edge of Starfish Gap.

The mermaids had told the truth. The gap was too narrow for anyone but a fairy. When she reached out her arms, Rani could touch both sides with her fingertips. The walls were rough.

Rani kicked harder, swimming down, down, down. Darkness began to close over her, and she stopped to look up. There, at the top, a long, long way up, were five beautiful mermaid faces. Oola held the light higher, and it cast its strange glow deeper into the gap and made eerie shadows on the walls.

"You're almost there!" Oola called. Her yellow-green hair floated around her face.

Rani looked down. She didn't feel as though she was almost there. She couldn't see the bottom and had no idea how far away it was. She wished she had thought to ask the mermaids how long she would have to swim to reach the floor of the gap.

But Rani wasn't afraid. She knew that the mermaids were waiting for her at the top. And she thought about how much fun they would have at the party.

It can be just like the Fairy Dance, Rani thought happily. *I'm sure the mermaids can do* flips in the water as easily as we can in the air. I'll teach them the steps to the Fairy Dance. And I can do it with them! It will be just like flying. In fact, it will be better!

Suddenly, a large rock loomed up before Rani. She squinted. There it was – the bottom of Starfish Gap! Sure enough, in the pale light cast by the seaweed lantern, Rani saw a small circle of gold set with a purple stone. She swam toward it.

But just as she reached for it, the light overhead went out.

Rani paused, holding still. *What happened?* she wondered. "Oola?" she called.

There was no answer.

Rani's heart thudded in her chest. She looked up. All she could see was deep black velvety darkness. "Voona?" she shouted. "Mara! Where are you?"

She waited, listening hard. Rani thought she heard the far-off sound of a giggle, but none of the mermaids shouted down to her.

Don't be afraid, Rani told herself. *There's nothing down here.*

Rani bit her lip. She knew she was alone. Still, the hairs on the back of her neck were standing on end, as though someone were watching her. A picture of the water snake flashed through her mind.

"There are no water snakes in Starfish Gap," Rani said aloud. Her voice sounded strange and echoey. How could she be sure there were no water snakes down there? And what if there was something worse? Like a giant crab? Or a fish with huge teeth?

"Oh, stop it," Rani scolded herself. "You're here to find the ring. Just get it and swim back to the top."

Swallowing hard, Rani reached out her hands. In a moment, her fingers touched the smooth, round ring. She hooked it over her shoulder and began to swim toward the top of the gap.

The seconds seemed to crawl by as Rani swam through the darkness. She couldn't tell how far she had come or how much farther it was to the top. Rani traced her fingers over her bubble necklace nervously. She reminded herself that she had plenty of air.

After what seemed like forever, Rani noticed that the walls around her had turned a dark, shadowy gray. A little higher, she saw a cluster of seaweed that looked like a bunch of trumpets. With another kick, Rani found herself at the top of the gap.

"I'm back!" Rani called. "I found it!"

But the mermaids weren't there.

7

Rani swam over to the yellow rock. The seaweed lantern was overturned beside it. Brilliant pink seaweed lay scattered where it had spilled from the shell.

"Oola?" Rani called. "Mara? I found the ring!"

There was no answer.

Rani's heart thumped wildly in her chest. She knew that the Mermaid Lagoon held many dangers. There were lightning eels, which gave off an electric shock whenever something touched them. There were the small but fierce saberfish, which had teeth that were longer than their fins. There were tusked Never sharks. These sharks usually left others alone. But when they were angry, they could be ferocious. And, Rani thought, there were probably other dangers, too. Ones she hadn't heard about.

Rani felt certain that the mermaids needed her help. *They wouldn't have left me alone unless something happened*, she thought.

Just then, Rani heard a faint splashing noise coming from somewhere above her. Without thinking, she began to swim toward the sound.

Rani swam as hard as she could. She kicked her legs and strained her arms. *If only I were a mermaid*, she thought, *I could swim so much faster!* A bed of clams snapped shut as she swam past. A small school of scissorfish chased each other through a red and orange coral forest. But the mermaids were nowhere to be found.

Finally, Rani stopped and looked around.

She wasn't sure which way to go.

Suddenly, there was a splash overhead. Then another splash, and a shriek. Rani looked up. Something large and silver was heading toward her. With a quick kick, she swam to the side. The silver thing dropped past her.

Then a flash of yellow-green darted by, like a ribbon in a fast breeze. It took a moment for Rani to realise that the yellow-green flash was Oola. She was chasing the silver thing.

Below her, Oola stopped. "I got it!" she shouted happily.

"Oola?" Rani called.

Looking up, the mermaid noticed Rani for the first time. "Oh, Rani, there you are!" she said in a rush. Oola swam over to the fairy and held out a large, heavy-looking silver mirror. "Look at what Peter Pan brought us,"

Oola said. "He stole it from the pirates – isn't that exciting?" She held it up and looked at herself.

Rani frowned. "I was worried that something had happened to you," she said.

Oola's yellow eyebrows drew together in confusion. "But why, silly fairy?" she asked. "What could happen?"

"Well… ," Rani began. Didn't Oola remember that she had gone down into the dark gap to get her ring? "I was down in Starfish Gap, and the light went out, and – "

Just then Voona called Oola's name.

Voona's head broke down through the surface of the water. Her wild orange and yellow hair floated around her face.

"There you are." Voona swam over, a pout on her full lips. "It's just like you to hog Peter's present all for yourself."

There was a splash, followed by two more. Mara swam over with two mermaids right behind her. "What do you think you're doing, Oola?" Mara demanded. "Give us the mirror!" She reached for it, but Oola held it out of reach.

"I was just talking to my fairy," Oola huffed.

My fairy? Rani thought with a frown. But all the mermaids had turned to look at her. Clearing her throat, Rani pulled the ring off her shoulder and held it out in both hands. "I found the ring," she said.

"Oh! My ring!" Oola dropped the mirror and looked at the golden ring with the glittering purple stone. She snatched it from Rani's hands and slipped it over her slender finger.

The other mermaids gathered around.

They oohed and ahhed over the ring. Rani couldn't help noticing that they seemed to have forgotten all about the mirror. *Just like they forgot about me*, she realised.

"I love purple," Mara said, running her hand through her blue and green hair. A comb with purple pearls was tucked into her locks.

Rani smiled. "So now we can have the party?" she asked eagerly.

But the mermaids didn't seem to hear.

"Well, yes, I suppose purple is all right," Voona said. She wagged her tail. "But it doesn't look very good on Oola."

Oola gaped at Voona. "It doesn't?" she asked.

Voona sneered. "It clashes with your hair."

Mara gasped. "She's right!"

"Purple doesn't go at all with green and yellow hair," pointed out a mermaid wearing a coral necklace that went perfectly with her red hair.

"Oh, how horrible!" said a mermaid with pink hair.

Oola's face turned a deep shade of green (that was how she looked when she was blushing). Yanking off the ring, she tossed it as far as it would go. It floated away and then down, down. It finally landed on a purple rock, where it bounced off... and dropped back down into Starfish Gap.

Rani stared at the gap in shock. The mermaids had sent her all the way down there for the ring, and now Oola had just thrown it back!

"Where did the mirror go?" Voona asked.

"I'll get it!" Mara called, starting toward

the bottom of the lagoon.

"Wait a minute," Rani said. "Wait."

Pausing, Mara looked up at Rani expectantly. "What is it?"

Rani didn't know what to say. The mermaids were not going to say they were sorry for sending her into the gap, or for leaving her there. Still, she wanted to think that she hadn't gone to all that trouble for nothing. "Well... uh ... was wondering ... When were we going to have the party?"

"Oh, that." Oola shrugged. "Well, we could have it now, I suppose."

Mara rolled her eyes. "But I wanted to look at the mirror!"

"We can have the par-tee quickly," Voona suggested. "And then we can look in the mirror."

Rani shook her head. "No, no - you

don't understand. We can't have a party right away. We have to get ready for it. You all have to learn the steps to the dance, and we have to make the food and plan the music. There's a lot of work to be done!"

All the mermaids were silent. Then, suddenly, they erupted into laughter. They hooted and guffawed, and chortled and giggled. Oola laughed until tears streamed out of her eyes, although, of course, no one could see that underwater.

"What's so funny?" Rani demanded.

"Hoo-hoo!" Voona said to the other mermaids. "The fairy wants to know what's – "

" – funny," Rani finished for her. "Yes, what's so funny?"

The mermaids laughed even harder. They chuckled. They howled. They snickered and snorted. Rani frowned. She liked the mermaids less and less by the minute.

"Mermaids don't work!" Oola finally said.

"But the work is half the fun," Rani protested.

Finally, the mermaids stopped laughing. They all looked at Rani as though she were crazy. Rani felt herself blush.

"I'll go get the mirror," Mara said, and she swam away.

"Would you like to look in the mirror?" Oola asked gently. Rani wondered whether the mermaid felt a little sorry for her.

"Don't be silly," Voona snapped. "Why would Rani want to look in the mirror? She isn't half as pretty as a mermaid! Besides, she's too little to hold it. She'd probably break it."

A wave of embarrassment rolled over Rani. She wished she could climb into a clamshell and hide. She couldn't help it that she didn't look like a mermaid. She was a fairy! And of course she wasn't as big as the mermaids or as graceful as they were in water. How could she be?

For a moment, Rani hoped Oola would disagree, but she only said, "You're right, Voona."

Mara swam up with the mirror in her hand. "I've got it!" she cried. Then she swam away, and the other mermaids swam after her. Rani was alone.

8

RANI SAT DOWN on a rock to think. "It looks like I don't really fit in anywhere." She sighed. She watched a fat blue blowfish dart behind a large tree of coral. "But I do like it down here. It's very pretty."

Soft light filtered through the water. It reminded Rani of the sunbeams that sifted through the Home Tree's green leaves. Two chubby striped brown flitterfish swam around and around a rock. Rani giggled. The fish looked like the chipmunks that lived in Pixie Hollow. A slow brown turtle swam past, as purposeful as a beaver on its way to build a dam in Havendish Stream.

Rani swam along, noticing other things that were like those in Pixie Hollow. There were corals shaped like twigs, a flying fish that looked like a sparrow, and anemones that looked like bushes.

Rani swam over to the flitterfish.

The two fish paused, gaping at her with huge round eyes. They were perfectly still, unable to decide whether Rani was dangerous.

"Hello," Rani said.

The fish darted away. In a moment, Rani couldn't even see them anymore. A cloud of bubbles floated where the fish had been.

"I guess they're shy," Rani said aloud.

Next, Rani paddled over to the brown turtle. Rani wasn't an animal-talent fairy. Still, she knew that the Havendish beavers were very friendly. "Excuse me!" Rani called. She tried to catch up to the turtle.

The turtle glanced at Rani out of the corner of his eye. He didn't stop or even slow down.

Rani tried again. "Pardon me. May I swim with you?"

The turtle kicked his flippers. He darted far ahead of Rani. She couldn't catch up. "Gee," she said to herself, "the creatures around here sure are unfriendly."

Just then, Rani caught sight of a patch of bright blue seaweed. It was shaking back and forth.

Is the seaweed caught in a water current? Rani wondered. *Or is this some strange underwater plant that can move by itself?*

Rani swam over to take a closer look. She stared at the seaweed, then reached out to touch it. The moment she did, a long snout popped out and batted her hand away.

Rani darted backward. The leaves of seaweed parted to show a golden pink sea horse thrashing about. His eyes were wild as he looked at Rani. He was still for a moment, then shook back and forth, rearing his head and whipping his tail.

Rani moved a little closer to the sea horse, and he thrashed again. He clearly was afraid of her. *Why doesn't he swim away?* Rani wondered.

"What's the matter, sea horse?" Rani asked in the tone of voice she had heard animal-talent fairies use when talking to a skittish animal. "Let me see," she said gently.

Rani felt a little nervous. If she had been in Pixie Hollow, she would have run for Beck or one of the other animal-talent fairies. *Then again*, Rani thought, *I am a water-talent fairy, and this sea horse is a water animal. Maybe I can help.*

Reaching out, she touched the rough surface of the sea horse's body. She expected him to buck, but he didn't. He was perfectly still. Rani looked at him more closely and saw that his tail was caught in a length of fishing line. The line was tangled in the seaweed, and the sea horse couldn't escape.

"Oh, you poor thing," Rani said. "You're all tangled up! Don't worry, I'll help you."

The sea horse eyed Rani nervously while she pulled at the stubborn knots with her tiny fingers. Once, she yanked a little too hard. The sea horse bucked.

Rani patted him. "Quiet down now, and I'll help you," she told the sea horse in a low voice. "We're almost there." The sea horse settled down, and Rani went to work on the knots again.

Over, under, through the loop. A tiny knot here, leading to a bigger knot there, then three more tiny knots. Finally, there were only two strands left. Rani pulled the fishing line away, and the sea horse was free.

"I did it!" Rani cried. "I did it!"

But she didn't get to celebrate for very long. The moment he was free, the sea horse raced away. He didn't even look back in Rani's direction.

Rani burst into tears. She couldn't help it. After all that work, even the sea horse didn't like her!

9

RANI CRIED AND cried, and her nose began to run, and then she got the hiccups. This was very uncomfortable underwater, and it only made her cry harder. It seemed as though no matter how hard she tried, nobody had any use for her!

Just then, Rani felt a gentle nudge at her hand. When she looked up, she saw the sea horse. He was carrying something in his mouth.

"Oh, hello," Rani said uncertainly.

Ducking his head, the sea horse dropped the object at Rani's feet. It was a large golden pearl. He looked up and nudged it toward her with his long snout. Then he looked at her again.

"A present?" Rani asked. "For me?"

The sea horse swam around in an excited circle. He nudged the pearl again, so that it was a little closer to Rani's feet. Rani reached down and picked up the pearl. It was large – about the size of an acorn. When Rani held it up, she saw that it glowed softly with its own golden light. Rani knew instantly that this was no ordinary pearl. It was magical.

"It's beautiful," Rani whispered. She turned to the sea horse. "Thank you."

The sea horse butted his head against her hand and turned so his back was facing her. He looked over his shoulder at Rani.

"Do you . . . do you want me to ride on your back?" Rani pointed to herself and pointed to the sea horse.

The sea horse turned another circle. He pulled up next to Rani. She took that to mean yes.

Rani giggled. "Well," she said, "I've ridden on the back of a dove. I guess I could ride a sea horse." Cradling the pearl in her left arm, Rani carefully climbed onto the sea horse's back. She leaned forward and wrapped her right arm around his neck. The moment he felt her holding on, the sea horse took off.

He swam quickly, headed for the deepest part of the lagoon. Rani clung tightly to his neck. She remembered flying with Brother Dove and felt a pang. She missed Brother Dove. She missed feeling the wind on her face.

The truth was, she missed Pixie Hollow.

Soon they entered an underwater garden. A small school of bright blue fish swept through an orange anemone. A yellow fish with purple spots scooted over a cluster of green seaweed. Everywhere she looked, Rani saw a rainbow of brilliant colours – purples and blues, greens and reds, spots and stripes and patterns she had never seen before.

"It's lovely," Rani whispered.

The sea horse seemed to understand what she had said, because he turned in a happy circle and moved forward through the garden.

In a few minutes, they left the underwater garden behind. The sea horse swam quickly toward a large shape in the distance. At first, Rani wasn't sure what it was. It looked like a mountain.

When they were a little closer, Rani gasped. Now she could tell what the mountain was!

"A sunken ship!" Rani exclaimed. She stared at the huge Clumsy ship as she and the sea horse swam past. It was larger than she ever could have imagined – even larger than the mermaid palace!

The sea horse swam up to a wall of rock with a small opening at the bottom.

"A cave?" Rani asked.

In answer, the sea horse ducked into the opening, which led to a long tunnel. It was very dark, but Rani wasn't afraid the way she had been when she was at the bottom of Starfish Gap. After all, she wasn't alone now. And she was starting to understand that the sea horse wanted to show her something.

A soft glow came from the end of the tunnel. As the tunnel brightened, Rani noticed that the walls glowed.

All at once, the tunnel opened up into an enormous cavern. It was so large that all of Pixie Hollow easily could have fit inside. Fingers of glittering rock dipped down from the ceiling of the cave.

"Oh, my," Rani said as she looked around.

Everywhere she turned, golden pearls like the one cradled in her arm lined the walls of the cave. The pearls reached right up to the ceiling.

"I'm the only fairy who has ever seen this," Rani said to herself.

Rani and the sea horse swam around, admiring the beautiful pearls. Finally, the sea horse looked over his shoulder at Rani.

"I hate to leave," Rani told him as they swam back through the tunnel. "It's just so beautiful here."

Rani thought he would take her back to the Mermaid Palace, or to the patch of seaweed where she had found him. Instead, he headed for the coral forest. "Why are we going here?" Rani wondered out loud.

The sea horse swam on. Soon, he stopped at a large cluster of seaweed. The seaweed parted and five tiny sea horses swam out, followed by another, larger sea horse. The tiny sea horses chased each other around Rani and her sea horse.

"Is this your family?" Rani asked as a tiny sea horse nibbled at her hair, then darted away. "They're so adorable!"

Rani slid off the sea horse's back and smiled at the sea horse family. They seemed so happy together. With a pang, Rani suddenly realised how much she missed her own family – the fairies.

"I wish I could go back," Rani said. "I wish I wasn't useless."

The sea horse nudged her hand.

"Thank you for showing me the lagoon," Rani told him.

Rani gave the sea horse a kiss on the snout. She waved and swam away. One of the tiny sea horses followed her for a while. But then he gave up and went back to his family.

Rani drifted, floating with the current. She wasn't sure what to do. She didn't want to go back to the mermaids. And she felt she couldn't go back to the Home Tree. Rani sighed.

Just then, something floated down from the top of the lagoon. It was silver, and for a moment Rani thought it might be Peter Pan's mirror. But once it got closer, Rani knew what it was. It was a bubble message, like the one she had sent Tink.

A small flitterfish swam over to it. He prodded the bubble with his nose. But the bubble wouldn't burst for anyone but the person to whom it had been sent. Rani touched the bubble, and Tink's voice tumbled out.

"Oh, Rani – wherever you are – please come back!" Tink begged. "Brother Dove has been looking high and low for you. Nothing seems right without you here. We need you. Please come back. Please."

Tink must have asked another water-talent fairy to help her make the bubble message.

She must really miss me! Rani thought. *And poor Brother Dove! He's been searching all over for me.* She felt terrible that she had made her friends so unhappy.

The flitterfish swam right past Rani. "I'm glad I came to the Mermaid Lagoon," Rani said out loud. "But I think it's time for me to go home now."

10

"RANI!" FIRA CRIED as she flew over to her friend and wrapped her in a huge hug. "You're – "

" – back! I know, isn't it wonderful?" Rani asked happily.

She looked around the fairy circle, where fairies were setting up for a party. *And it's going to be in my honour!* Rani thought dizzily. The fairies were so happy that she was back that Queen Clarion had declared a holiday. All the talents were busy preparing.

There was even a water fountain. Everyone in the water talent had worked on it, including Rani. Six large spiders wove a thick curtain around the fountain so the water-talent fairies could work in secret. Pixie Hollow was buzzing with the news that

Rani's party fountain was extraspecial.

I never knew that everyone cared so much, Rani thought. She stroked the soft feathers at Brother Dove's neck. He had hardly left her side since she had returned.

"Rani's back, and she's had an adventure," Tink put in.

"I know – the whole Home Tree is buzzing with the story," Fira said. "No one can wait for the big party tonight. Everyone wants to hear Rani talk about the mermaids and her trip down Havendish Stream. Did you really battle a – "

" – water snake?" Rani grinned. "I sure did."

Fira's eyes widened. "Wow. I always knew you were brave, but... " She shook her head.

"Well, I *was* kind of frightened," Rani

admitted.

"*You* were frightened?" Tink exclaimed. "Think about how frightened we were when we couldn't find you!"

Rani frowned. "I wish I hadn't worried you. I'd fly backward if I could."

Tink grabbed her friend's hand. "I'm just glad you're home."

"I don't think any fairy has ever seen what you have, Rani," Fira said.

It was true. And while some of her adventure hadn't been much fun – like the water snake, the trip down Starfish Gap, and the mermaids, who had barely seemed to care when Rani went back to say good-bye to them – other parts, like meeting the sea horse, had been wonderful.

"Rani is special," Tink said. "There's no other fairy like her."

Just then, Vidia flew up to them. "Oh, Rani, darling, I'm so glad you're back," she said with a tight little smile. "Pet, everyone was worried *sick* about – "

" – me?" Rani said. "Don't tell me *you* were worried, Vidia."

The corners of Vidia's mouth twitched up into an almost-smile. "Sweet child, I see we're having a little party in your honour," she said. She batted her long, dark eyelashes. "Are you going to 'help' with the fountain again?"

Tink's face turned red with anger. Rani spoke up. "Actually, Vidia, I *did* help with the fountain. Would you like to take a look?"

Without another word, Rani hopped onto Brother Dove's back. She buried her hands deep in his soft feathers and held on tightly as he took off. A moment later, she was flying through the air. The wind was cool against her face.

"Everyone, come quick!" Tink shouted. "Rani is going to unveil the fountain!" Brother Dove wheeled above the fairy circle as fairies poured into the clearing. They came from all directions. Even Queen Clarion came flying from the Home Tree. Everyone wanted to see the fountain.

Rani let Brother Dove turn twice more before she gave him the signal. With a sudden plunge, the bird dove toward the spider threads that held up the curtain. Rani pulled a small rose thorn from her hip pocket. As Brother Dove passed the threads, she cut them one by one.

Rani broke the last thread. The curtain fluttered gently to the ground.

The fairies gasped. For a moment they were silent. Then, suddenly, they burst into applause.

The fountain was lit from the inside with a glowing golden light. The water seemed to sparkle with gold dust as it showered down the sides of the fountain. It was beautiful.

Rani and Brother Dove had spent the whole morning flying back and forth between the Mermaid Lagoon and Pixie Hollow. With the help of her sea horse friend, Rani had collected six of the magical golden Never pearls from the cave at the bottom of the lagoon and brought them back to use in the fountain. The pearls glowed just as prettily in freshwater as they did in the lagoon.

Below Rani, the fairies' applause went

on and on.

Tink put her fingers into her mouth and let out a loud whistle. Showers of sparks rained from Fira's hands as she clapped. Rani blushed, but she couldn't help giggling. There was only one fairy who wasn't clapping. Vidia looked positively green.

Brother Dove fluttered his wings and landed beside Tink. Rani was instantly surrounded by fairies. Terence thumped her on the back. Tink caught Rani in a tight hug. The light-talent fairies had a million questions. Everyone was smiling and congratulating Rani at once.

Once the hubbub died down, Vidia recovered her smile. "Well, Rani. I see that you managed to do what the light-talent fairies couldn't," she said. She gave Fira a sideways look. "How did you – "

" – light up the fountain?" Rani finished for her. "Oh, it's easy, if you know how." She grinned at Tink, who winked.

"Maybe I can't put the top jet on the fountain," Rani added, "but it looks as though I'm talented after all."

Vidia stuck her nose in the air. "I don't know if I'd say *that*, darling," she replied. And with a toss of her head, she flew off.

"She sure is a pain," Fira said as she watched Vidia fly away.

Tink waved her hand. "Don't worry about her," she said. "We have a party to go to."

Rani smiled. "That's right," she agreed, thinking how happy she was to be back in Pixie Hollow, where she belonged.

"Besides, we've just found another of your talents, Rani," Tink said. "A really useful one."

"What's that?" Rani asked. She was pleased to have yet another talent.

Tink grinned. "You light up Pixie Hollow!"

Rani smiled. "With the magical pearls," she said.

Tink shook her head. "No, Rani," she told her friend. "You light it up all by yourself."

Join Tinker Bell, Prilla and all
the other Never Fairies in
the next Disney Fairies book...

Beck and the
Great Berry Battle

Here is a fairy-sized preview
of the first chapter!

Beck

and the

Great

Berry

Battle

1

A SQUIRREL PERCHED on a log paused while chewing on some seeds. He watched as two tiny Never fairies zipped past him, side by side.

"Oh, Beck," one of the fairies said to the other as they flew. "Thank you so much for coming with me." She looked terribly worried. "We just don't know what to do. A baby raccoon turned up in the gardens this morning, and he ate all the strawberries out of Thistle's strawberry patch. And then he started digging up Rosetta's mint! We chased him off, but he didn't go far. Now he's sitting on a tree stump by Havendish Stream. He won't budge. And none of the other animal-talent fairies can understand a word he's saying!"

Beck smiled. "Don't worry, Latia," she said. They were nearing Havendish Stream. "We'll figure it out."

Latia breathed a sigh of relief. "Well, if any fairy in Never Land *can* figure it out, it's you, Beck!"

Every fairy in Never Land agreed: Beck was one of the finest animal-talent fairies in Pixie Hollow. She loved being around animals, from the tiniest insects to the largest mammals. Oh, sure, snakes could be a little grumpy. Skunks were hard to read. And hawks, of course, were just plain dangerous. But all in all, she loved feeling a part of the animal world. Sometimes Beck secretly wished that *she* were an animal!

Like all the animal-talent fairies, Beck

had a gift for talking to animals. Birdcalls, mouse squeaks, squirrel and chipmunk chatter – they were just noises to the other fairies. But to animal-talent fairies, those different noises held meaning. To them, animal sounds were as clear and easy to understand as words and sentences.

Beck was especially good at talking to baby animals, perhaps because she was so playful and lighthearted. She loved playing hide-and-seek with the young squirrels and having somersault contests with the baby hedgehogs. Even when an animal was too young to speak, Beck could understand it. Queen Clarion said Beck had empathy and could sense animals' emotions. When those emotions were strong enough, Beck felt them, too.

So when a baby raccoon parked himself on a stump and refused to move, everyone thought of Beck right away. The animal fairies sent Latia to fetch Beck because she was a forest-talent fairy and knew the quickest ways to get through Pixie Hollow.

An easy five-minute flight later, the two fairies came to Havendish Stream. A dozen animal-talent fairies were hovering around a tiny raccoon, who sat on a tree stump clutching a stalk of Rosetta's mint.

"Beck's here!" Latia called, and all the fairies turned.

"Oh, thank goodness!" cried Fawn, one of Beck's best friends. She drew Beck closer to the tree stump. "Beck, you've just got to help. This poor little fella won't budge. We don't even know where he *came* from." With a push from Fawn, Beck found herself right in front of the baby raccoon. He raised his head and whimpered.

"Hello there," Beck said in Raccoon. "I'm Beck. What's your name?"

The little raccoon let out another whimper. Then he buried his face in his paws and rubbed his nose in the stalk of mint he had picked from Rosetta's garden.

"Oh, don't cry!" Beck said. She flew up and stroked the top of the raccoon's furry head. The raccoon rocked back and forth – and Beck's lip started trembling. The baby raccoon was so sad and so scared that Beck was starting to feel sad, too. She straightened her back, cleared her throat, and forced herself to cheer up. If she didn't watch out, soon she'd be crying as hard as the little raccoon, and then where would the fairies be?

"Hey, now," said Beck, smiling. "Don't cry, my friend. Why would you cry when you could be playing a game with me?"

Raising his head, the little raccoon looked at Beck for the first time. She smiled encouragingly and patted his nose. "That's right," she said. "I know the perfect game for us to play. It's called Find the Fairy!"

With that, Beck took off at top speed. She looped around behind the raccoon and tapped him on the shoulder. "Here I am!" she cried. The raccoon squeaked in surprise and turned around, but Beck was already gone.

The little raccoon peered up at the sky, trying to find her. Meanwhile, Beck quietly landed by the stump and tiptoed around to the front, where the raccoon's paw rested on the edge. She reached up, tweaked his toe, and cried, "No, *here* I am!" then flew up to face him again.

The little raccoon let out a chittering noise: raccoon laughter. All the fairies smiled at each other. Beck had done it again!

Beck grinned. She was so glad that the little fellow was feeling better. "That's a good game, isn't it?" she said. "Now let's start again. My name is Beck. What's wrong?"

There was a pause, and the fairies held their breath. Then the raccoon replied. To the fairies who didn't speak Raccoon, what he said sounded like "Grak!"

But Beck understood him.

"Lost!" was what the raccoon said. Beck realised that he was so young, he still spoke Raccoon baby talk. He stared at Beck with wide eyes. "Lost!" he said again.

"Oh, dear. Well, where do you live?" Beck asked.

"Live... ," the raccoon started.

"Yes?" Beck asked encouragingly.

"Live... ," he said again. He looked down

at the mint stalk he still held. He raised his paw and shook the mint at Beck. "Live *here!*" he said. "Live... in *mint.*"

"Huh," said Beck, switching out of Raccoon. She looked at the fairies who were gathered around. Everyone looked as confused as she felt.

"What did he say?" asked Latia.

"He said... that he lives... in *mint,*" Beck told her. "But that doesn't make any sense!"

"In mint?" replied Latia thoughtfully. "I wonder if he means – Oh, Beck! I know where he lives!"

"Remember when Rosetta planted her mint patch a few years ago?" Latia asked Beck. They were flying through the woods, with the raccoon trailing after them. "Well, she asked me to find her some wild mint seeds from the forest, because she likes their flavor. So I got her some seeds from a big old wild mint patch at the base of a hollow tree right on the edge of Pixie Hollow. I just *bet* his family lives in that tree!"

"You must be right," agreed Beck. "That would explain why he was so interested in Rosetta's mint patch to begin with. It must have reminded him of – "

"Home!" cried the little raccoon, and took off running. Beck and Latia looked up, and sure enough, there was the big hollow tree. And playing in the mint leaves at the bottom of the tree was another baby raccoon. She was about the same age as Beck's little friend – who was in such a hurry to get to the tree that he barrelled into her. The two young raccoons tumbled in a heap at the foot of the

hollow tree, squeaking happily.

It was obvious that the little raccoon was home.

Soon, it had all been sorted out. Beck explained everything to the baby raccoon's mother, who thanked her again and again. She even offered Beck an old, slimy leaf of cabbage (rotten cabbage is a delicacy to raccoons).

"Thank you so much, but it's really not necessary," Beck said. She waved good-bye to the baby raccoon, and then she and Latia flew off in the direction of the Home Tree.

As they were flying over a thicket, Beck spotted Grandmother Mole coming out of an underground tunnel. "Oh, Latia, why don't you go on without me?" Beck suggested. "I want to pay a visit."

Grandmother Mole was the oldest

female mole in Never Land, and a very dear friend. She and old Grandfather Mole had no children or grandchildren of their own. But they were known throughout Pixie Hollow as Grandmother and Grandfather Mole.

"Hello, Grandmother," Beck said in Mole. She landed at the animal's side.

"Beck? Is that you?" asked Grandmother Mole in a series of grunts and nose whistles.

"Yes, it's me," Beck replied. "I was just flying by and I saw you. How's everything underground?"

"Oh, just fine," Grandmother Mole replied. She told Beck all about the moles' latest tunneling projects. "But there's much more exciting news than that," she added. "One of our own just had babies – four beautiful and perfect baby moles. You should come by and see them sometime. You can teach them to play peekaboo."

Beck smiled. "That sounds wonder – "

Just then, old Grandfather Mole climbed out of the tunnel opening – and bumped right into Beck. "Oops!" he said with an embarrassed chuckle. He squinted in Beck's direction. "Pardon me, sir! Wasn't watching where I was going, I guess!" He chuckled again.

Then Grandfather Mole waddled off. Grandmother Mole giggled at his blunder – calling Beck "sir." Beck couldn't help giggling, too. All the moles were nearsighted. But Grandfather Mole, well, he was practically blind.

After saying farewell to Grandmother Mole, Beck flew east, to the Home Tree. She smiled as she flew. She was filled with a sense of wellbeing. Maybe it was from helping the baby raccoon get back home. Maybe it was the happy news of the baby moles' birth. Whatever it was, it made Beck feel, at that moment, that all was well with the world.

Then, just as Beck flew over the river, she heard it. A cry. A cry for her? Was someone calling her name? As she slowed, it got louder.

"Beck! Be-e-e-e-eck! Wait! Wait up!" the voice called.

Beck stopped and hovered in midair. Where was the call coming from? She looked to the left. She looked to the right.

She turned to look behind her – and saw a young hummingbird headed straight for her, at full speed. He was screaming at the top of his lungs. "Beck! Help! He-e-e-e-elp!"

Collect all the Disney Fairies books

Discover the story of the Never Fairies in Fairy Dust and the Quest for the Egg

Coming soon!